COMPANY'S COMING

COMPANY'S
COMING

BY

ARTHUR YORINKS

ILLUSTRATED BY

DAVID SMALL

HYPERION BOOKS FOR CHILDREN
NEW YORK

LIBRARY OF CONGRESS CATALOGING-IN-PUBLICATION DATA

Yorinks, Arthur.

Company's coming / Arthur Yorinks;

illustrated by David Small.

p. cm.   Summary: Chaos erupts when Moe and Shirley invite

some visitors from outer space to stay for dinner with the relatives.

ISBN 0-7868-0500-5(tr) — ISBN 0-7868-2433-6 (lib)

[1. Extraterrestrial beings—Fiction. 2. Humorous stories.]

I. Small, David, 1945– ill. II. Title.   PZ7.Y819 Co 2000

[E]—dc21   99-56159

Visit www.hyperionchildrensbooks.com

For Shirley
—A.Y.

For Sarah
—D.S.

On the day Shirley had invited all of her
relatives to dinner and Moe, her husband, was
pleasantly tinkering in the yard, a flying saucer quietly
landed next to their toolshed. Moe was surprised.
"Shirley!" he yelled.

Shirley joined Moe on the patio.

"Moe, you had to buy *that* barbecue? It's too big,"
she complained.

"Shirl, it's not a barbecue," Moe said.

Suddenly, a small hatch on the saucer opened
and out walked two visitors from outer space.
"Greetings," they spoke in English. "We
come in peace. Do you have a bathroom?"

Stunned, Shirley replied, "Down the hall
and to the left." The foreigners nodded graciously
and walked into the house.

"How could you let them into our house!"
Moe was upset.

"Did you see those helmets? Those ray guns?
They'll vaporize us!" Moe was very upset.

"Shhush, they're coming," Shirley whispered. "Stay calm. Be polite. Maybe we can make friends with them."

"What a lovely house you have," the strangers commented. "What do you call this place?"

"Bellmore," Shirley politely answered. The visitors nodded.

"We're from away. Far away. And we've been traveling for years on our way to the next galaxy—"

"How about a sandwich, you must be hungry,"
Shirley nervously interrupted. "Would you like to
stay for dinner?"

"Gee!" they replied. "We'd love to. We'll
return at six o'clock." The spacemen went back to
their ship and flew off. Moe and Shirley ran into
the house.

"Are you crazy! The cousins are coming tonight. Why did you invite *them* to dinner?" Moe asked. "They'll atomize us. Bellmore . . . the whole Earth is doomed, I tell you!" Moe was hysterical.

"Moe, Moe, take it easy. They look like nice boys," Shirley said. "Come, help me make the potato salad."

But Moe had other thoughts. Saying he had
to wash his hands, he went upstairs and called
the FBI. The FBI called the Pentagon. And
the Pentagon called the Army, the Air Force,
and the Marines.

At a quarter to six, the house was surrounded.

Inside, the cousins sat, panicked.

"Act natural," Shirley told her relatives. "Be nice.
So they look a little different, I'm sure they're friendly,"
she said, as she served the appetizers.

"Don't worry," Moe added. "If those aliens make
one false move, they've had it! So relax."

Moe heard a humming and ran to the window.
"They're here!" he yelled.

The doorbell rang. Everyone froze. Cousin
Etta fainted.

"I'll get it," Shirley called. She went to the door. "Hello, hello, come right in," she greeted the men from outer space. They were carrying a box.

"How about a drink, some soda? Are you
tired? It's getting late, if you leave now you'll just
miss the traffic." Moe tried to usher them out.

"So, guys, what's new, have you been to Venus yet, I hear it's hot in the summer," Cousin Sheldon the loudmouth asked. The spacemen sat.

"Well, we're on our way to check out a new planet. Our population has grown so quickly that we must branch out and find new places to live; know what I mean?"

"Sure, we know what you mean," Moe blurted out. "An invasion—we're doomed," he whispered to Cousin Harriet.

"Dinner!" Shirley called.

"Oh, please, before dinner, we have something for you. It'll knock you out." The visitors presented their box.

"It's a bomb! It's gas! It's a laser!" Etta yelled and then fainted again. Soldiers burst into the house. Tanks pointed their guns.

Shirley gingerly began to unwrap the gift. "We weren't sure if you had one of these," the men started to say.

Shirley interrupted. "It's a, it's a, it's a—" The cousins were paralyzed.

"It's a, it's a," Shirley continued. Moe was sweating from head to foot. "OH!" Shirley blurted. Etta, Moe, and Sheldon fainted.

"It's a *blender*!" Shirley declared.
"And we don't even have one."

"We thought you'd like it. And it was on sale!" The spacemen beamed. Shirley went over and kissed them both. "Let's eat!" she said.

Luckily, Shirley had made extra spaghetti and
meatballs. The cousins, the soldiers, the pilots,
the Marines, the FBI men—everyone sat down
and had a delicious meal; from soup to nuts.